# THE MONSTER GANG

## Felicity Everett

## Designed by Maria Wheatley

## Illustrated by Teri Gower

Edited by Harriet Castor

Language and Reading Consultant: David Wray
Education Department, University of Exeter, England

Series Editor: Gaby Waters

First published in 1995 by Usborne Publishing Ltd, Usborne House, 83-85 Saffron Hill, London EC1N 8RT, England. Copyright © 1995 Usborne Publishing Ltd.

Meet Micky Brooks and his friends.

Here he is with his little brother, Ben.

Ben

Micky

Tas

This is Tasneem. She's called Tas for short.

Here's Ellie with her dog, Goldie.

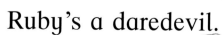

Ellie

Goldie

Ruby's a daredevil.

Lee

Ruby

Lee collects comics. He and Micky do swaps.

It was Saturday. The friends were on their way to Ellie's house to play.

Ben splashed through every puddle in his big red boots.

Micky and Lee kept out of his way.

Tas zoomed past on her bike.

Ruby was doing an amazing stunt. She still had the grazes from the one she did yesterday.

Ellie was
trying out her
new skipping rope.

Which do you think
is Ellie's house?

5

First they played
hide and seek.

Then they went up
to Ellie's room and
tried out all her games.

They drew
masses of pictures.

Then they
were bored.

6

Suddenly
Ruby had an idea.

Let's start a gang.

What made her think of it?

7

They all thought a gang was a brilliant idea.
But what should they call it?

Everyone          thought          hard.

Then they each wrote down a name . . .

. . . and put
it into Tas's
cycle helmet.

Ben closed his eyes,

dug deep,

and picked one out.

The Monster Gang

Let's meet tomorrow at our treehouse.

I ♡ GOLDI

Yes, and we could all dress up.

What name did he pick?

The next day
six monsters met
at Micky and Ben's
treehouse.

Some were
scary. Some
were funny.

It was hard
to tell who
was who.

They began
to climb up the
rope ladder.

Climbing
was tricky in
monster clothes.

The monster with the
red boots led the way.
Can you tell who it is?

11

To get in a
monsterish mood,
the gang put up
some scary pictures.

Then they made
cobwebs out of string
and bats out of paper.

It was only
half past eleven,
but they were already
feeling hungry.

Luckily Lee and Ruby
had brought a picnic.

What was there
to eat and drink?

13

Ben gave out the drinks.
    He tried to guess who each monster was.

Grazed knees...

I'd know that hair anywhere.

Those glasses look familiar.

And you like reading comics...

14

At last, Ben thought he'd cracked it.

Can you tell who each monster is too?

15

The last monster had to be Ellie.
But you couldn't tell.

They all agreed
her costume was the best.

They gave her a
badge to wear.

Ogulugulug.

she said, spitting
cake crumbs
everywhere.

She was a special monster
now. Can you tell why?

17

Now they had their leader, they could get on with some other gang business.

First they tried to think up a secret sign. They tried lots of different ones.

This is the one they chose.

Next the gang made up some rules.

Everything to be written in code.

Gang meetings to be top secret.

Masks to be worn at all times.

Their leader wrote them down.

Which rule is Micky breaking?

Just then, they heard a call from outside.
It sounded like Ellie, but how could it be?
Ellie was already here.

They rushed to the doorway and looked outside.

It was Ellie.

Sorry I'm late. I had to take Goldie for a walk.

But if Ellie was down there, then who was the leader of the Monster Gang?

They rushed back inside the treehouse.
The mystery monster had vanished.

Suddenly, Ellie
saw a note lying
on the floor.

said Ellie. But
Ruby thought she
knew the answer.

When they held the note
up to a mirror, they could
read it. Turn the page to
see if you can read it too.

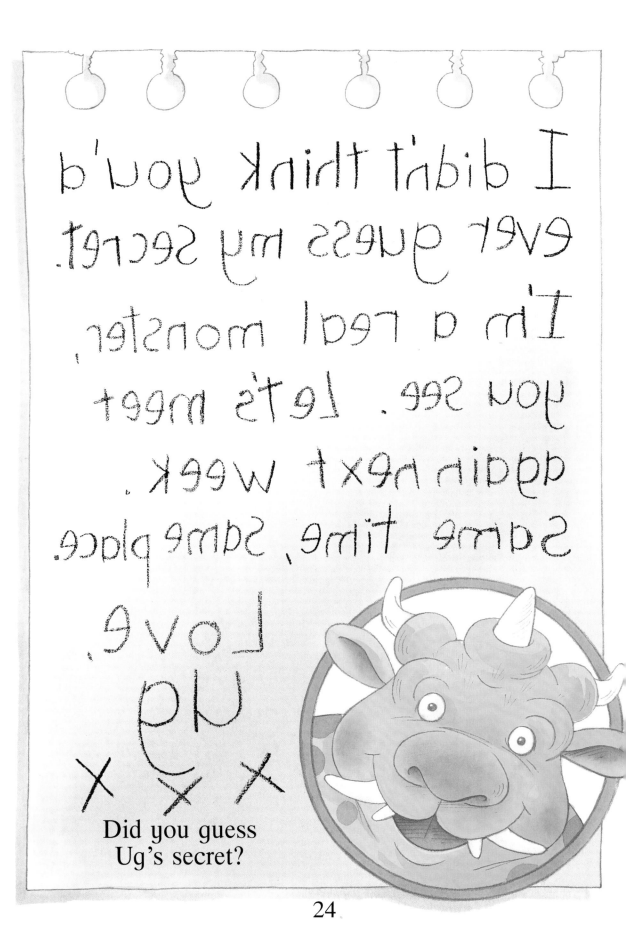

I didn't think you'd ever guess my secret. I'm a real monster, you see. Let's meet again next week. Same time, same place.

Love,

Ug

XXX

**Did you guess Ug's secret?**

# THE CLUMSY CROCODILE

Felicity Everett

Designed by Maria Wheatley
and Alex de Wolf

Illustrated by Alex de Wolf

Language and Reading Consultant: David Wray
Education Department, University of Exeter, England

Series Editor: Gaby Waters

Everglades was no ordinary department store.

It sold things that you just couldn't buy anywhere else.

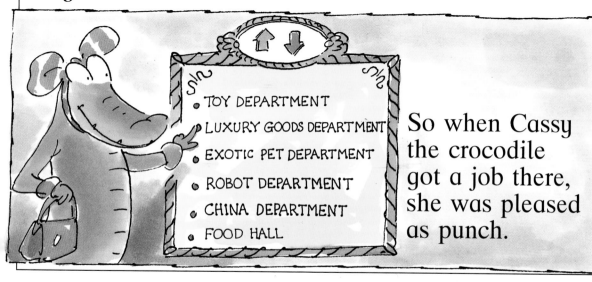

- TOY DEPARTMENT
- LUXURY GOODS DEPARTMENT
- EXOTIC PET DEPARTMENT
- ROBOT DEPARTMENT
- CHINA DEPARTMENT
- FOOD HALL

So when Cassy the crocodile got a job there, she was pleased as punch.

But things didn't go quite
as well as Cassy hoped.

In the china department,
she packed sixty cups
and saucers,

in a bottomless crate.

In the toy department,
her tail knocked the
Toytown Express
off the rails.

In the food hall,
she upset
the salad.

I'll see you
in my office.

And that upset
someone very
important indeed.

Who was he?

29

The boss shook his head.

The boss sighed.

He told Cassy to go to the Luxury Goods department first thing on Monday morning.

Who were the Greedy Boys?

Cassy was determined to make a fresh start.

All day Sunday she worked on her stacking,

wrapping,

and serving
with a smile.

Then she put on her Everglades badge
and admired herself in the mirror.

CASSY
MAY I
HELP
YOU?

What did the badge say?

On Monday morning, Cassy was the first to arrive in the Luxury Goods department.

The security guard was finishing breakfast.

The guard told her to keep her eye on the Everglades Emerald.

Why was the Everglades Emerald so precious?

Cassy wasn't the only one with her eye on the Everglades Emerald.

What was Nigel worried about?

The Greedy Boys didn't realize it,
but Cassy <u>had</u> heard the whistle.
Why?

Cassy thought the whistle sounded like the Toytown Express.

She dashed off to check that no one was messing with the train.

But her tail got caught
on a pearl necklace.

The
pearls
went
everywhere.

And so did
the Greedy Boys.

Which department was Cassy heading for?

Thinking they were customers, Cassy tried to help them up.

But she stumbled on the emerald...

...and crashed into a table.

42

What was on the table?

But the boss saw the emerald lying on the floor,

and quickly put two and two together.

No need. You've saved the Everglades Emerald and caught the Greedy Boys.

How did he know they were the Greedy Boys?

That afternoon the boss gave a party for Cassy at Everglades.

EVERGLADES

The whole town was there.

Except for the Greedy Boys. They were safely behind bars.

46

The Mayor presented Cassy with a special medal.

What did it say?

The next day Cassy went to work at Everglades as usual.

But from now on she could play the latest video games,

eat chocolates and drink pink lemonade.

What was her new job?

48

# THE INCREDIBLE PRESENT

Harriet Castor

Designed by Maria Wheatley

Illustrated by Norman Young

Language and Reading Consultant: David Wray
(Education Department, University of Exeter, England)

Series Editor: Gaby Waters

Lily lived in a big, old, dusty house.

She lived there with her Great Aunt Maud, who knitted things.

The house had spiders under sofas and beetles between bed legs.

But Lily liked it.

It was Lily's birthday morning.

She jumped out of bed,

got dressed

and ran downstairs.

There she found a note.

Happy Birthday Lily.
follow the arrows to find your presents

Beside it was a small arrow.
Lily followed the arrow upstairs.
The trail took her all around the house.
Which rooms did she look in?

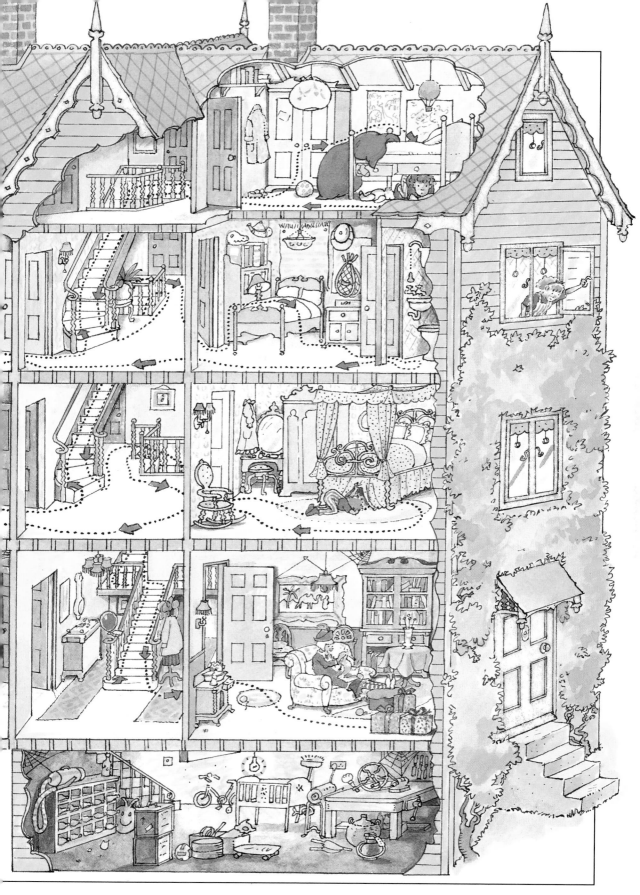

Lily ended up in the
sitting room.
Great Aunt Maud
was there.

Lily's presents
were there, too.

She "SQUISHED" them and "SQUEEZED" them.

Then she lined them up,

and piled them high.

Next, she got out her X-RAY glasses.

Giraffe

Toy Garage

Super long range telescope

What could she see?

At last, Lily opened her presents.

The first present wasn't a super long range telescope.

The second present wasn't a giraffe.

The third present wasn't a toy garage.

THANKYOU
Letter
Writing Paper

Then Lily saw one last present.

To Lily,
Great Aunt
Maud's House.
(from somewhere on)
the high seas.

Where had it
come from?

The parcel was from
Lily's Ma and Pa.

Ma and Pa were explorers.
Lily didn't mind when
they went away.
They always came
back with exciting.
stories to tell.

They had
set off on an
expedition to
the jungle.

They were due
back soon.
Lily hoped it said
on the parcel when
they'd be home.
Did it?

Will be back
in time for
your birthday.
Love Ma
and Pa xxx

59

Lily wondered what Ma and Pa had sent her from their travels.

A dinosaur tooth?

A rainbow hamster?

An ice cream plant?

She opened the parcel. Inside was a small bag.

There was a label on it.

The Anything Bag. Ask for anything you want, reach inside and there it will be~

Lily tried it out.

I'd like some crayons please.

There was something strange about the crayons.

What was it?

Lily wrote a list of everything she wanted to ask the bag for.

Then she noticed a second label.

Pet snail
Bubble bath with the biggest bubbles in the world

55 Bowls of Pink icing

P.S. you can only ask for six things.

There were five choices left. Lily thought hard.

She hated making her bed every morning, so she asked for

A bed making robot.

But it didn't do quite what she wanted. What did it do?

Lily's fourth choice was

A witch's kit with real spells in it.

pong

poo

wiff

Witch's cat with real smells in it

But the bag must have heard her wrong.

What did she get instead?

65

Lily hated having cabbage for dinner,
so next she asked for

A zapper that turns all your greens into chocolate ice-cream.

Lily tried it out.

It worked!

But everything green
had been zapped,
including

Great Aunt
Maud's hat

and most of
her garden.

Lily, do
something!

Then Lily had
an idea.

Happy
Birthday
Lily,
love Ma
and Pa.
xxx

Can you guess what it was?

For her last choice,
Lily asked for

Ma and Pa to come home.

They arrived in a flash,
and Lily told them what had happened.

We'd better put the bag into reverse.

Pa turned the bag inside out.

Then Ma said something complicated.

For you asked Lily that everything back take please, bag dear.

Can you figure out what it meant?
(Clue: try reading the sentence back to front.)

The grass was grass again.

The robot and his beds had gone.

Lily couldn't smell the cat anymore.

And she couldn't hear any alien babies squawking.

Lily hoped this meant they weren't going away again.

Then she spotted something that told her the answer.

What was it?

Soon all was quiet.

You'd never have guessed
what a strange birthday
it had been.

Except that
Great Aunt Maud
was never quite
so fond of her
green hat again.

It always made her
ears a little sticky.

# THE DINOSAURS NEXT DOOR

Harriet Castor

Designed by Maria Wheatley

Illustrated by Teri Gower

Edited by Emma Fischel

Language and Reading Consultant: David Wray
(Education Department, University of Exeter, England)

Series Editor: Gaby Waters

Stan lived at number 3, Green Street.

Mr. Puff lived next door.

From the outside, Mr. Puff's house looked a little strange.

Inside, it was even stranger...

Mr. Puff's house had rooms
full of very strange things.

Some were machines
that he had built.

76

Some were bits and pieces
that he had collected.

Some were things
that even Mr. Puff
couldn't explain.

Mr. Puff had a cat, too.
What was her name?

One day, Stan knocked
on Mr. Puff's door.
Mr. Puff opened it and said:

Hello, Stan.
There's something
I want you
to see.

Stan followed him inside.

Mr. Puff dived under the table.

He brought out a large basket.

Eggs?

Not just any old eggs. They're...

Dinosaur eggs. Handle with care.

But Stan already knew what they were. Do you?

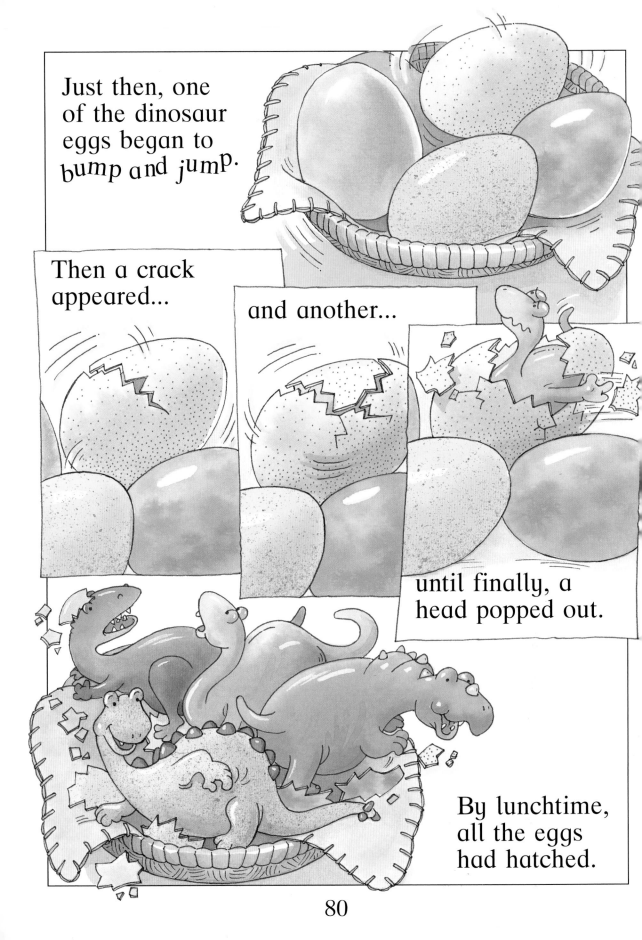

Just then, one of the dinosaur eggs began to bump and jump.

Then a crack appeared...

and another...

until finally, a head popped out.

By lunchtime, all the eggs had hatched.

Mr. Puff fetched a book.

What did the book say dinosaurs ate?

Stan wasn't sure what sort
of dinosaurs all these were.

He put out some salad
and some cat food,
just in case.

During the next three days,
the dinosaurs grew...

and grew.

They're getting
very fierce.

On the fourth day,
Mr. Puff was worried.

Then he had an idea.

He rummaged in
one of the rooms
and dragged something out.

What was it called?

Mr. Puff gave Stan the hose
and told him to point it
at a dinosaur.

Then he pushed a lever.

There was a cloud
of starry smoke.

The dinosaur
had gone away.

Or had it?

Can you see where it has gone?

85

Stan and Mr. Puff set to work on the other dinosaurs.

One was in the garden.

Another was in the kitchen.

The last one was in the bathroom.

But just as Mr. Puff pushed the lever, the dinosaur lunged at Stan.

Stan slipped, and the hose flew out of his hand.

What did Stan slip on?

The smoke cleared. Stan couldn't believe his eyes.

Everything around him was enormous... except Mr. Puff.

Eek! The Size-o machine has shrunk us as well as the dinosaur!

They heard a...

roar

Look at those teeth. Run!

Suddenly,
the dinosaur
turned its head.

What has the
dinosaur seen?

89

Then they moved the hose into place.

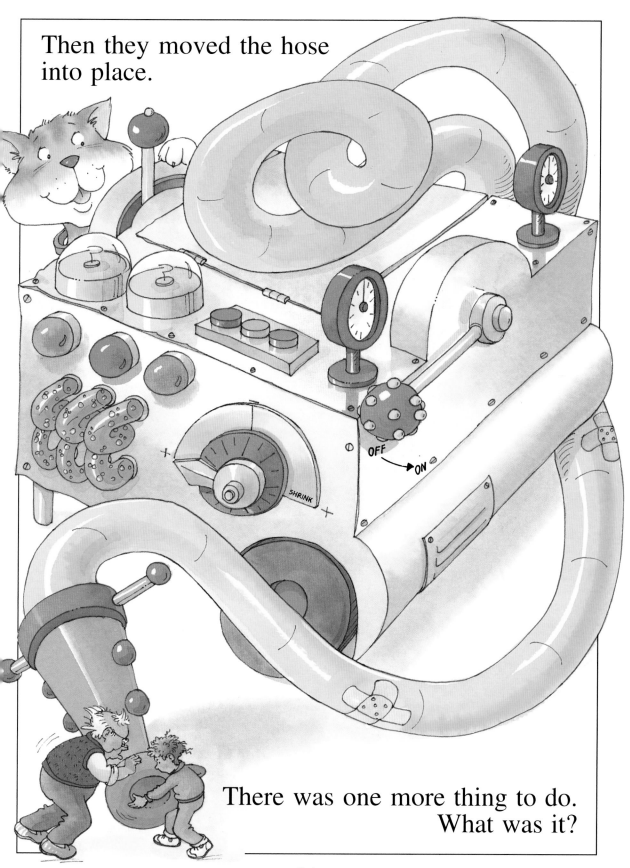

There was one more thing to do.
What was it?

The lever was high above
them. Stan climbed onto
Mr. Puff's shoulders.

OFF

SHRINK

But he couldn't
shift it.

Then they both
climbed up and
bounced on the lever.

But that didn't work either.

Just then,
Amy jumped up onto
the Size-O machine.

What is
Amy doing?

I think
she's seen that
cat food.

Can you see what is
going to happen?

Down went the lever.

There was a cloud of smoke.

At last Stan and Mr. Puff were back to normal size.

Mr. Puff and Stan went
to find all the dinosaurs.

I think
they would make
nice pets.

Stan wasn't so sure.
In fact, he was quite
glad to go home.

Mr. Puff offered Stan
a dinosaur to take home.
But Stan chose
something else instead.

What was it?

Stan didn't tell anyone about the dinosaurs next door - or about his narrow escape.

You're a very clever cat.

But whenever he saw Amy, he always went out to give her a saucer of milk.